WHEN I GROW UP I WANT TO BE, LIKE THE BRAVE MEN

OF

TUSKEGEE

LaVon
Stennis Williams

ILLUSTRATED BY
RANA DIGI PAINT

two bee
PUBLISHING

OMAHA, NEBRASKA

Two Bee Publishing
A division of LSW Strategies, LLC
1941 So. 42nd St. Suite 502
Omaha, NE 68105
twobeepublishing@gmail.com

Paperback ISBN: 978-1-7322440-1-6
Hardcover ISBN: 978-1-7322440-2-3
Kindle ISBN: 978-1-7322440-3-0
EPUB ISBN: 978-1-7322440-4-7

Library of Congress Cataloging Number: 2018941341
Cataloging in Publication Data on file with the publisher.

Illustrated by Rana Digi Paint
http://instagram.com/ranadigipaint
Design by Concierge Marketing Inc.

Printed in the United States of America
10 9 8 7 6 5 4 3 2

Dedicated to

Sergeant Kyle W. LeFlore,

the Tuskegee Airmen,

the brave men and women who have
fought and served our country,

and to my grandchildren, Aniya,
Ryleigh, Maxwell and Brandon.

Hi! My name is Brandon Dean and I am 8 years old. I love to read, do science projects, and I really love to do math. I already know all my multiplication tables up to 12!

Everyone tells me I am very smart for my age. I think it's because I love to learn new things. I read for 20 minutes every day—Sunday, Monday, Tuesday, Wednesday, Thursday, Friday, and Saturday. By my math, that's over 100,000 words a year!

I can do a lot of things, but I really want to fly! Not like a bird or butterfly, but like the men my Papa told me about called the Tu-ske-gee Airmen. (Wow! That's hard to say.) The Tuskegee Airmen didn't really fly. They flew planes and that's what I want to do when I am older.

Sometimes, I dream that I am a Tuskegee Airman flying way up in the air. Sometimes I get my airplane out and run around the yard pretending to fly.

I have lots of books about planes and pilots. Pilots are the people who fly planes. I think I have more books on planes, pilots, and the Tuskegee Airmen than any other kid in the whole wide world, including my best friend Kyle Wayne. Someday, when he grows up, he wants to go into the Army. We love to pretend we are flying planes just like the Tuskegee Airmen.

When I am not flying planes, I am usually reading books about planes and pilots with Papa. He's my favorite person to read books with. Papa was the first one who read a book to me about the Tuskegee Airmen.

They were African American men who became pilots and helped our country fight in World War II. They look just like my papa, daddy, my best friend Kyle Wayne, and me, but older. Well, Papa looks older than they do. Papa told me that many people did not think these men could fly because they were African American. That never made sense to me.

Stars indicate the states Tuskegee Airmen came from.

During World War II, President Roosevelt issued Executive Order 8802 in June 1941, directing that African Americans be accepted into job-training programs, paving the way for the Tuskegee Airmen to earn their wings and go into battle.

Papa said, "One day, Brandon, these men were given a chance to learn how to fly, and they went to a college in Alabama called Tuskegee. They were smart, just like you, and I bet when they were your age, they could read, and do math and science, too."

"Really, Papa? Could I be a Tuskegee Airman now?" I asked.

"The Tuskegee Airmen came from all over the country to learn how to fly planes. There were 16 men from right where you live in Omaha, Nebraska, and they trained for over 7 weeks!" Papa said.

"That's a lot of weeks, Papa!"

Papa and I learned a lot of things from my books, like the Tuskegee Airmen learned to fly at a field called Moton Field, which was near Tuskegee College. An African American teacher named Charles Anderson taught them how to fly planes.

One day, President Roosevelt's wife, Eleanor Roosevelt, came to visit Moton Field. She wanted to show that people were wrong about African Americans not being able to fly. She got in the plane with Charles Anderson, and he flew her from Tuskegee, Alabama, all the way to Mobile, Alabama. She was not afraid. She helped prove to the world that African Americans could fly too. I wish I could have been there. I would have gotten in the plane with them.

When the men finished their first training at Moton Field, they were sent to another place called Tuskegee Army Airfield. Once they finished at Tuskegee Airfield, they got their wings, which meant they were officially pilots.

Papa explained that they did not get real wings because people do not have wings. They got a pin on their jacket that proved that they were now pilots. They were very brave, and ready to help fight in the war.

Another important Tuskegee Airman Papa said I should know is Lieutenant Colonel (Loo·ten·ent Ker·nal) Benjamin O. Davis, Jr.

He was the first African American to be a commanding officer at Tuskegee Airfield, but he did not go to Tuskegee College like the other men. He went to West Point, a very important training school. He was the only African American at West Point and no one would even talk to him.

Lieutenant Colonel Davis was very strict with the Tuskegee Airmen. He wanted them to be the best because the whole wide world was watching them to see if they would be good pilots. The Tuskegee Airmen worked hard and proved that were great men and pilots and were very important in the fight against our enemies during the war.

FACTS ABOUT THE TUSKEGEE AIRMEN

- The Tuskegee Airmen flew planes called P-40 Warhawks and P-47 Thunderbolts. But the most famous planes were called P-51 Mustangs.

- When the pilots of the 332nd Fighter Group painted the tails of their P-51 Mustang planes red, they became known as the "Red Tails" or the "Red Tail Angels".

- The Tuskegee Airmen flew 15,533 combat sorties with 1,578 missions.

- They destroyed 112 German aircrafts in the air and 150 German planes on the ground.

- From 1942 through 1946, 992 pilots graduated from the program and received their silver pilot wings. In all, there were between 14,000 to 16,000 Tuskegee Airmen, because any person who assisted the pilots during the time of the training program was considered a Tuskegee Airman.

- Not all of the men in the pilot training program got their silver wings. If the military only needed a certain number of pilots, then some of the men would "wash out". This did not mean they failed, it meant they did not make the cut because the military did not need any more pilots. It was an honor to be a part of this great program whether they received their wings or not.

I knew I wanted to be a Tuskegee Airman too, but Papa said I couldn't be one because they graduated their last class a long time ago and the program has ended. Papa said I could still be a pilot and fly like the Tuskegee Airmen.

AFRICAN AMERICAN AVIATION HISTORY

Even before the Tuskegee Airmen program started, African American men and women were learning how to fly, and some even had their own schools to teach other African Americans how to fly.

James Banning was the first African American Aviator to earn a pilot's license. He was born in 1899, and went to college in Iowa majoring in Engineering. When he first tried to enroll in a pilot's training program, he was not allowed to enroll because of his race, but eventually he was allowed to enroll in a US Army Pilot Program. In 1929, he received his pilot's license from the US Department of Commerce.

Bessie Coleman was the first African American woman in the world to earn a pilot's license. Flight schools in the United States would not let her apply because of her race, so she taught herself how to speak French and moved to France to enroll in flight school there. She earned her license from a well-known school of aviation in just seven months.

Willa Beatrice Brown was an American aviator. She was the first African-American woman to earn her pilot's license in the United States. She was also the first African-American officer in the US Civil Air Patrol and the first woman in the United States to have both a pilot's license and a mechanic's license. Along with Cornelius Coffey, she co-founded the Cornelius Coffey School of Aeronautics, which was the first private flight training academy in the United States owned and operated by African Americans. She trained hundreds of pilots, several of whom would go on to become Tuskegee Airmen.

23

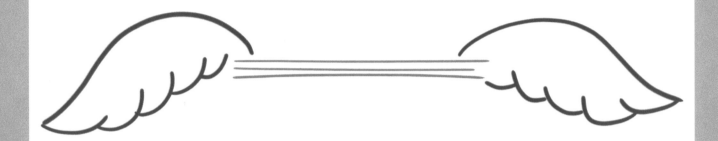

The stories of the African American Aviators
who lived long before me prove that I can
become a pilot when I grow up too.

WHAT DO YOU WANT TO BE WHEN YOU GROW UP?

WORD SEARCH FIND THESE WORDS:

(ANSWERS ON THE NEXT PAGE.)

```
N G B V O J T I F Z H L M Z A N X Y L W
F M F V M O Z Q F U U S H M S E S G B V
V C L D F L I G H T M M Z S D G O Z P V
Y A Y O S K Q Q E O D E I W M Y R Z R F
H F I C T M I S S I O N W W K U T J D B
W Z N I B X I F W O R L D W A R I I E P
I Q G O A W W Z R T L G P I U S E W P S
F J K L I C E N S E M I L R E D T A I L
A T V D R A D R Y C X Q U Q V U H G L L
L H W A M Y E O Z H M Y P Q E P V N O H
A M V N E G C P S N J C V U N N G X T L
B O K T N I X M O O I H W H G P Z W W K
A T P Z C B D N Y L L S F K I A Y G O F
M O U P A V I A T O R I W A N A G T L E
A N Q W T U S K E G E E I R E C M J I T
U F Q F F A Z P E Y R N N M E H A A P F
W I R V J Z Y K N P M X G Y R P Z X P V
I E J S G P Z B Q X A A S C I E N C E F
K L N O J Y A M U S T A N G N J N E Q A
L D G C T J J M F T H X C T G C N X X S
```

TUSKEGEE	FLYING	LICENSE	MUSTANG
AIRMEN	SCIENCE	ARMY	WINGS
ALABAMA	MATH	SORTIE	REDTAIL
PILOT	TECHNOLOGY	MISSION	WORLD WAR II
AVIATOR	ENGINEERING	FLIGHT	MOTON FIELD

If you are interested in learning more about the Tuskegee Airmen, visit www.TuskegeeMuseum.org, www.TuskegeeAirmen.org, or www.TuskegeeAirmenNebraska.com

```
N G B V O J T I F Z H L M Z A N X Y L W
F M F V M O Z Q F U U S H M S E S G B V
V C L D F L I G H T M M Z S D G O Z P V
Y A Y O S K Q Q E O D E I W M Y R Z R F
H F I C T M I S S I O N W W K U T J D B
W Z N I B X I F W O R L D W A R I I E P
I Q G O A W W Z R T L G P I U S E W P S
F J K L I C E N S E M I L R E D T A I L
A T V D R A D R Y C X Q U Q V U H G L L
L H W A M Y E O Z H M Y P Q E P V N O H
A M V N E G C P S N J C V U N G X T L L
B O K T N I X M O O I H W H G P Z W W K
A T P Z C B D N Y L L S F K I A Y G O F
M O U P A V I A T O R I W A N A G T L E
A N Q W T U S K E G E E I R E C M J I T
U F Q F F A Z P E Y R N N M E H A A P F
W I R V J Z Y K N P M X G Y R P Z X P V
I E J S G P Z B Q X A A S C I E N C E F
K L N O J Y A M U S T A N G N J N E Q A
L D G C T J J M F T H X C T G C N X X S
```

CPSIA information can be obtained
at www.ICGtesting.com
Printed in the USA
BVHW062204041021
618116BV00003BA/10